for sure! for sure!

For Darcie and Tim.—SC

To the fairy twins, Tallulah and Beatrix.—MW

Translation copyright © 2004 by Mus White.
Illustrations copyright © 2004 by Stefan Czernecki.

Published 2004 by August House LittleFolk, P.O. Box 3223, Little Rock, Arkansas 72203 501-372-5450
www.augusthouse.com

Published simultaneously in Canada by TRADEWIND BOOKS, LTD.

The acrylic paintings are rendered on watercolour board. • The text of this book is set in Gill Sans.

Book design by Elisa Gutiérrez

10 9 8 7 6 5 4 3 2 1

LIBRARY OF CONGRESS CATALOGING-IN-PUBLICATION DATA
· ·

Andersen, H.C. (Hans Christian), 1805-1875
[Der er ganske vist! English]
For sure! for sure! / a tale by Hans Christian Andersen ;
illustrated by Stefan Czernecki; translation by Mus White.
      p.   cm.
Summary: When a chicken who has accidentally lost a feather jokes that she
looks more gorgeous the more she plucks herself, her comment spreads
throughout the coop and town and takes on a life of its own.
ISBN 0-87483-742-1 (alk. paper)
[1. Fairy tales. 2. Gossip-Fiction. 3. Chickens-Fiction.]
I. Czernecki, Stefan, ill. II. White, Mus. III. Title.
PZ8.A542Fo 2004
[E]-dc 22   2004040991
· ·

Colour Separations by Bridgeport Graphics • Manufactured in Korea

for sure! for sure!

Hans Christian Andersen

illustrated by Stefan Czernecki

translated by Mus White

AUGUST HOUSE
Little folk

LITTLE ROCK

"It's a shocking story!"

clucked one chicken who lived in the section of town where the scandal didn't take place. "It's a hideous thing that happened in the chicken coop! I'm afraid to sleep alone tonight! It's a lucky thing that so many of us sit close together on this perch!" Then she told a tale that made the feathers of the other chickens stand straight up and the rooster's comb droop down. It's true, for sure!

We'll start at the beginning,
and that beginning started
on the other side of town
in a chicken coop. The sun
went down, and the chickens
flew up. One of the chickens
—she was white-feathered and
short-legged—laid her eggs like
clockwork. For a chicken, she was
quite respectable in every way.

Right off, after she settled to roost on her perch, she began to groom her feathers with her beak. And then a tiny feather fell off.

"Out it popped!"

she giggled. "The more I pluck myself, the more gorgeous I look." She said it all in good fun. In fact, among the chickens she was known to be the silly one, but of course she was also very prim and proper. Then she fell fast asleep.

It was dark all around. Chicken sat next to chicken.

Only the one who sat closest to the silly chicken hadn't yet fallen asleep. She heard everything, and she heard nothing, just as you are supposed to do in this world when you want to keep the peace. But, of course, she had to tell her best friend: "Did you hear what she said? I'm not naming any names, but there's a chicken who wants to pluck herself bare to look pretty!

If I were a rooster, I would give her the cold shoulder, without a doubt!"

Right above the chickens sat Mama Owl with Papa Owl and their little owlets. They have sharp ears in that family. They heard

every word
that the
chicken
below said,
and they
rolled their
eyes, and
Mama Owl
fanned herself
with her
wings.

"Just don't listen! Of course, you did hear what was said, didn't you? I heard it myself with my own two ears, and you have to hear a lot before your ears fall off! One of the chickens has so forgotten how a chicken ought to behave that she sits and plucks all her feathers off, right there in front of the rooster!"

"Shhh,"

said Papa Owl. "That kind of talk is not for children's ears."

"I just have to tell it to the owl next door! She is such a nice owl!" said Mama Owl before she flew off.

"Hoo! Hoo-hoo!"

Mama Owl and her friend hooted and howled right down to the pigeon house below them. "Have you heard! Have you heard! Hoo-hoo! There's a chicken who has pulled all her feathers out just for the sake

of the rooster! She is freezing to death! That's if she isn't frozen stiff already.

Hoooo!"

"Where? Where?"

cooed the pigeons.

"Down there in the yard next door! I've as good as seen it for myself! It's almost too ugly a story to tell! But it's quite true, for sure!"

"For sure, we believe it word for word!" the pigeons said while they cooed down to the chicken yard.

"There's one chicken, yes, some even say there are two, who have pulled all their feathers out so that they will stand apart from the rest of the chickens.

Just to catch the rooster's attention! **That's a**

risky game to play!

You could catch a cold and drop dead from fever. Both of them have probably bitten the dust by now!"

"Wake up! Wake up!"

crowed the rooster flying up on the fence. Drowsy and quite droopy-eyed, he shouted anyway: "Three chickens have collapsed from a broken heart over a rooster!
They have plucked all their feathers out! It's a nasty scandal.

I don't want to keep the story to myself. Spread the news!"

"Spread the news!"

squealed the bats, while the chickens clucked, and the roosters crowed.

"Spread the news! Spread the news!"

Then the story bounced from chicken coop to chicken coop, and at last back to the place where it actually began.

"Five chickens," it was told, "have all plucked their feathers out to prove which one of them wasted away the most because of their love for the rooster. Then they pecked at each other in a bloody battle until they all keeled over dead, bringing shame on the good names of their families. Not to mention causing a huge loss to their owner!"

Of course, the chicken who had lost the loose little feather didn't recognize her own story, and since she was an upright chicken, she said: "I can't stand that sort of chicken! There are so many of them around, though! That's why you shouldn't ever keep quiet. I, for one, will do whatever it takes to make sure the story gets into the newspaper. Then the news will spread right across the country.

That's exactly what those chickens, and their families, deserve!"

The story did get into the paper, and it did get into print, and it's all true: one little feather can grow into five chickens!

For sure! For sure!

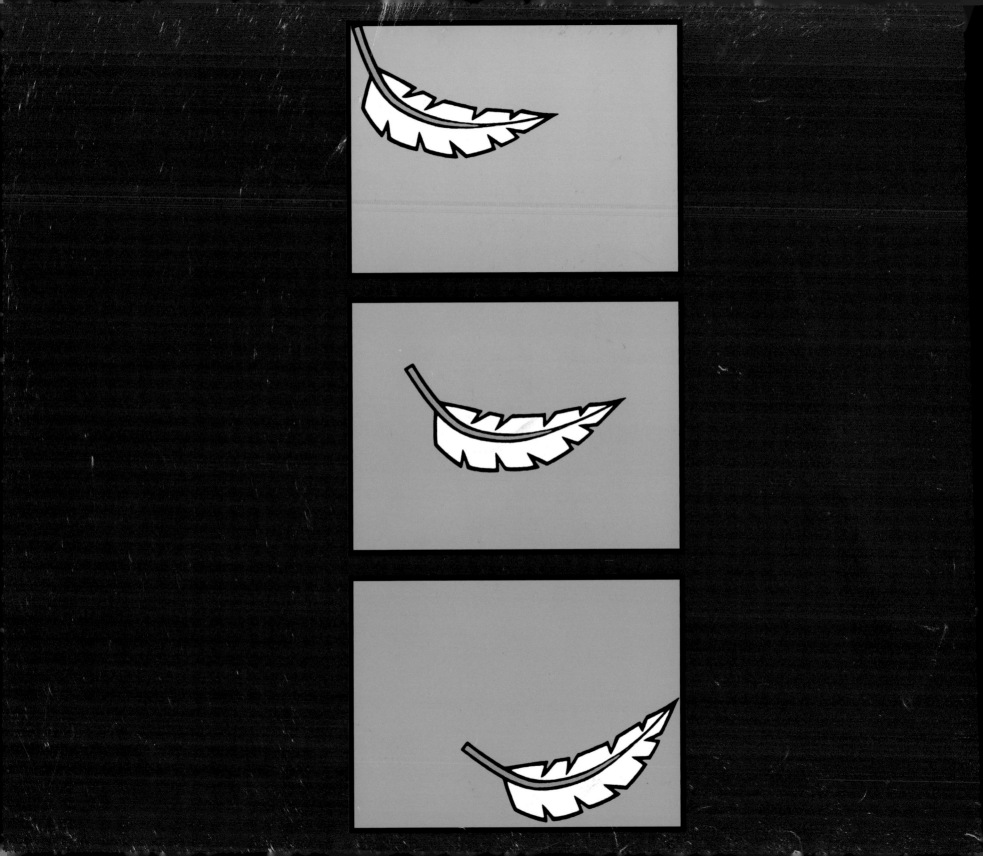